David Vozar

D1401197

M.C. TURTLE and the HIP HOP HARE

a happenin' rap

Illustrated by Betsy Lewin

A Picture Yearling Book

Published by
Bantam Doubleday Dell Books for Young Readers
a division of
Bantam Doubleday Dell Publishing Group, Inc.
1540 Broadway
New York, New York 10036

ISBN: 0-440-41394-X

Reprinted by arrangement with Doubleday Books for Young Readers

Printed in the United States of America

September 1997

10 9 8 7 6 5 4 3 2 1

This book is dedicated to the kids…
including the class of Yo! 3R,
my nieces Laura and Sarah,
and my daughter, Ariane.
—D.V.

To my nephews Jesse and Wyatt.
—B.L.

The Challenge

The Hip Hop Hare was dissing all around,
Rapping that he is the fastest critter in town.

"All you animals are no competition.
There's no way, under any condition,
I can lose a race to anyone running.
You know, I'm not joking and I'm not funning."

"Wait a minute!" came a soft voice drawling.
"I'm M. C. Turtle, which stands for 'mostly crawling.'

"I hate to be the one who's interrupting,
But all of my friends you are corrupting.
How can you say you're the fastest in motion?
Where did you get that ridiculous notion?"

More animals came out of their houses—
All the squirrels, birdies, the chipmunks and mouses—

Saying, "Why don't you race? That will decide it.
The winner will be the fastest, the loser must abide it.
We'll all come out and you can race tomorrow.
One will be happy, the other in sorrow."

The rabbit laughed, and said, "I will beat him,
Rush him, crush him, annihilate and defeat him."

M. C. Turtle tried to stop the hare's boasting,
But now has to race and get a roasting.
He will have to run really fast and hustle,
And hope the rabbit falls or pulls a muscle.

The Race

This big ol' bovine comes up to the mike,
Makes this long moo sound
That means something like

"Get set to go now!"
Then the starter cow
Pulls on the trigger
And the gun goes *pow*!

Hare's feet go zipping, there'll be no tripping,
And in a second
This guy's a-ripping.
The zooming hare jokes,
"Guess who wins this, folks?
Hope you're not rooting
For turtle slow-pokes."

Hip Hop laughs and says, "This is too easy—
I feel really great,
Not a bit wheezy.
This running is fun
And this here bun-bun
Certainly knows that
He's already won."

Then the rabbit churns and turns up the speed—
Not just a little,
But more than he needs.
In a short while
He gets a broad smile
'Cause he's out in front
By more than a mile.

START

All this time the turtle's really going,
Traveled four feet and
Says without slowing,
"I go as I go—
It's all that I know.
I know that I'm slow,
But I go as I go."

Down the Road

Way out in front, the big-ear guy hops.
He's getting bored and wants to stop.
He's looking 'round for a place to chill
When he spots something and, oh, what a thrill.

He spies some fine chicks who flirt and tease
Make him turn three hundred sixty degrees—
Chicken Little, Henny Penny,
Just to count two chickens of the many.

He puts on the brakes and burns his toes.
The giggling fowl ask him to pose.
The birds all cluck and they click their shots,
But their bright flashes make his eyes see dots.

The birds said, "You'd better get going
Or else the race you'll be blowing."
Hip Hop replied, "Yo! I'm so fast,
If I raced a jet, it would come in last."

But he had enough of their flashes.
He says "Ciao!" and then he dashes
Down the road, where he hears a sound.
It was shaking the trees, road, and ground.

There were speakers and a real def stage
And a rap band that's all the rage—
Little Bo Peep and The Sheep band—
And Hip Hop is one of their biggest fans.

M.C.'s been crawling for all this time,
Going along repeating his rhyme:
"I go as I go—
It's all that I know.
I know that I'm slow,
But I go as I go."

The Finish Line

Bo Peep had the hare's head spinning.
Hip-hop dancing, he lost track of winning.
His brain was saying he should go,
But the beat had his feet and they said, "No!"

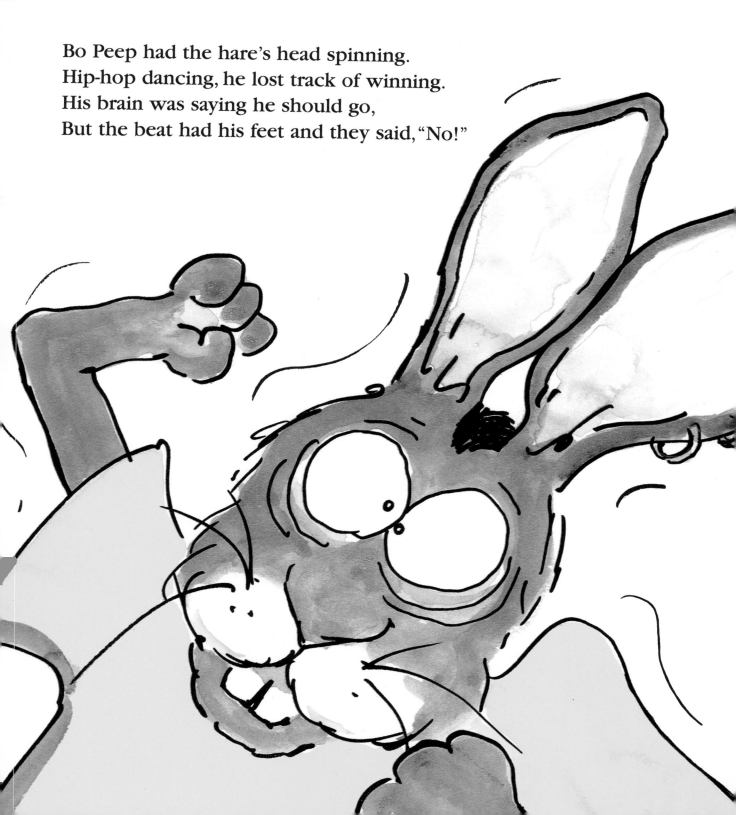

The shell-guy's been climbing uphill—
He's creeping along by sheer force of will.
But when he got up to the crest,
He started rolling down head, feet, and chest.

Fast and faster M.C.'s traveling,
Dreams of winning in his head unraveling.
Maybe he won't do the losing—
"M. C. Turtle must mean 'mostly cruising.'"

Hare was dancing, enjoying the song,
When he sees a blur go by, rolling strong.
He sees it's his reptile foe—
There is no time left, he just has to go.

Bunny runs as fast as he can,
But turtle is really rolling strong, man.
The finish line is just ahead—
Hip Hop's not first but the turtle instead!

FINISH

M.C. steps up to get his prize.
As he climbs the stairs, the crowds realize
That this may take quite a while.
They all go home and the turtle smiles.
"I go as I go—
It's all that I know.
I know that I'm slow,
But I go as I go."

The Next Day

The next day, Hip Hop sees the shell-guy,
Runs up to him and begins to cry,
"You go as you go, I know, I know.
You won the race even though you were slow.
But I'm better than you, and you I will beat!
Let us arm wrestle now. Come on, let's compete!"

M.C. said, "No! *I'll* pick the contest,
And then we'll know who is the best.
Here is the challenge I put to you.
Here is the thing that we're going to do.
Let's see who can go without any bragging.
That means no boasting-rabbit windbagging."

Hip Hop just didn't know what to say—
That was the point as he walked away.
As M.C. watched the dejected hare,
He thought to himself, "I won the race fair.
Now I am the new fastest critter in town—
So I think I'll spread *that news* all around!"